Robot's SPECIAL DAY

Mary Ray

Illustrated by
Tony Sumpter

OXFORD
UNIVERSITY PRESS

OXFORD

UNIVERSITY PRESS

Great Clarendon Street, Oxford OX2 6DP

Oxford University Press is a department of the University of Oxford.
It furthers the University's objective of excellence in research, scholarship,
and education by publishing worldwide in

Oxford   New York

Auckland   Cape Town   Dar es Salaam   Hong Kong   Karachi
Kuala Lumpur   Madrid   Melbourne   Mexico City   Nairobi
New Delhi   Shanghai   Taipei   Toronto

With offices in

Argentina   Austria   Brazil   Chile   Czech Republic   France   Greece
Guatemala   Hungary   Italy   Japan   Poland   Portugal   Singapore
South Korea   Switzerland   Thailand   Turkey   Ukraine   Vietnam

Oxford is a registered trade mark of Oxford Universi~~ ~~~~~
in the UK and in certain other countries

Text © Mary Ray 2003

The moral rights of the author have been asser   **JS**

Database right Oxford University Press (make

First published in this edition 2007

British Library Cataloguing in Publication Data

Data available

ISBN 978-0-19-915171-4

1 3 5 7 9 10 8 6 4 2

Mixed Pack (1 of 6 different titles): ISBN 978-0-19-915168-4
Class Pack (6 copies of 6 titles): ISBN 978-0-19-915167-7

Printed in China by Imago

Contents

Chapter 1

Robot Gets a Job

The only space was next to Chelsea Carter. Robot didn't want to sit next to Chelsea Carter.

"Sit down, Robot," said his teacher, Miss Turner.

Robot's real name was Robert. But when he was little, he couldn't say "Robert" properly. So he ended up as Robot. And now that's what most people called him.

He sat down.

"We've got a special visitor today," said Miss Turner. "The Mayor's coming to see us!" She gave her warning look. "So you'll all be good, won't you?"

Robot felt as if she meant just him. Chelsea Carter smiled. She thought she was always good.

Miss Turner began to call the register.

Robot thought about the visit. A
mayor sounded important. Like a king.
Only with a gold chain instead of
a crown. And a big car.

Chelsea Carter pushed Robot hard.
"Wake up! You've got to say 'Yes,
Miss Turner.'"

"That's enough Chelsea," said Miss Turner. "Leave Robot alone."

That told her, thought Robot. He smiled at Miss Turner. Miss Turner smiled back.

"I need someone to take the register. Will you do it, Robot?"

Robot could hardly believe his ears.
She was asking him to take the register to
the office!

Chelsea Carter couldn't believe her
ears either.

"I could go with him."

"No," said Miss Turner." This job is
for Robot."

She handed him the register.
An important job! On his own!
Robot beamed.

Chapter 2

Where is Everyone?

"Straight there and straight back," said
Miss Turner.

Robot set off. He loved helping. It was
easier than writing and number work.
Mostly, he didn't get chosen. He'd never
had an important job.

In the hall, Mrs Peters' class was round
the piano. Robot tiptoed carefully.
His trainers squeaked.

"Robert Weston!" barked Mrs Peters.
"Stop making a noise in my class!"
It wasn't fair! He hadn't made a noise.

Robot went through to the entrance hall. There was no one there. Just the fish, drifting round their tank.

The Head's room was empty. So was Mrs Gohill's office. It was spooky. Where was everybody?

Robot put the register on Mrs Gohill's desk. On her computer, a spaceship turned slowly. Robot gazed at it. He'd like one of those. And a telephone. And a special tray for paper clips and pens.

Robot suddenly felt scared. He shouldn't be there on his own. What if Mrs Mason, the Head, found him? He'd get told off! He dashed out of the office.

Robot skidded to a halt in the entrance hall. A lady and a man were by the fish tank. They had smart suits – and enormous gold chains.

Chapter 3

A Good Idea

"Hello," said the lady. "We wondered where everyone was. Let me guess. You're the caretaker."

Robot grinned. "She comes after school."

"You must be the Head, then!" said the lady.

Robot giggled. "No! I'm Robot."

The lady laughed. "Wonderful! A school run by a robot!" And she shook Robot's hand.

Robot tried to look grown up. But he didn't know what to say. She looked like his Nan. Except for the chain, of course.

He never had important visitors at home. Just people like Mrs Went from next door, and his Nan. They were always calling in for cups of tea.

Suddenly, he knew what to do.
"Would you like some tea?"
he asked.

"That would be lovely!" said the lady. "You show us the way."

In the big hall, Mrs Peters was playing the piano. Robot put a finger to his lips.

"We mustn't make a noise," he whispered. "Or Mrs Peters will tell us off."

He walked in time to the music, with his head up. Chelsea Carter had never had a job as important as this! The Mayors followed him.

In Robot's classroom, Miss Turner had her back to the door.

Robot went straight to the Home Corner.

Just then, Chelsea Carter shouted in her "I'm-telling" voice, "Miss Turner! Robert Weston's got two Mayors!"

Miss Turner spun round.
The lady Mayor smiled.

"I hope you were expecting us? Robot
asked if we'd like some tea."

She squeezed into the Home Corner
and perched on a chair.

"I'm dying for a cup."

"If you're sure?" said Miss Turner.

"Certain," said the lady Mayor.

And she told the man to sit down, too.

Chapter 4

"At Home"

Robot dived into the cupboard. He found
a teapot with no lid. He also found two
saucers, a mug and a cup with a chewed
handle.

Chelsea Carter pushed him out of the
way. "You need the table cloth, silly."
Chelsea Carter thought she was more
important than anyone else in the
whole world!

Miss Turner came over.

"Chelsea, Robot can manage." And she led Chelsea Carter back to her seat.

"I've got a teapot like that at home!" said the lady Mayor. "Can I pour?" And she helped Robot to make the tea.

Robot found a plastic number-work cake. And even the man said, "Mmmm ... Delicious."

While they had tea, the lady told Robot about being a Mayor. And the children brought their work to show.

Suddenly Mrs Mason swept into the class. A man with a camera rushed along behind her.

The whole class stopped.

Mrs Mason was very red in the face!
She took the lady Mayor by the hand.

"I'm SO sorry! I didn't know you'd
arrived. Then this reporter turned up, and
Mrs Peters told me..."

Mrs Mason gave Robot such a look!

"Robot's made us feel SO at home!"
said the lady Mayor. "I think he should
meet all your visitors. It's been our
best visit ever!"

Chapter 5

Famous!

It was Robot's best day ever.

He found out that the lady was the Mayor. The man was her Deputy. Their chains weren't made of real gold. And the Mayors came in a Jaguar with a flag on the bonnet, and a driver in a peaked cap.

The lady Mayor wanted to have her
picture taken with Robot. It was in
the newspaper:

Hextable Herald

Mayor takes tea with Robot!!

Mayor of Hextable, Maggie Walmsley,
and her Deputy, Reg Todd, had a
surprise welcome when they visited
Hextable Primary School.

The Mayors really enjoyed their visit
"We met Robot and his friends and
had a lovely tea," said Mrs Walm...
Then we went round the other c...

The paper said about Robot's name.
And it said how much the Mayors
enjoyed their visit, too. Miss Turner put
it on the wall with a notice saying:
"Robot's Special Day!"

And there wasn't a word about
Chelsea Carter.

About the author

I'd been trying to write this story for ages, but I couldn't get it right. Then I remembered a boy I used to know, called Robot, who loved helping. And the story fell into place. I don't know anyone called Chelsea. But I've known a few children like her! As for important visitors… It helps if they like children as well as being important.

My husband Tony did the illustrations for the book.

I took this photo in our garden